Fifteen Shades of Time

Fifteen Shades of Time

Philip Charter

KONSENSUS NETWORK

ISBN 978-9916-749-37-1 Hardcover
 978-9916-749-38-8 Paperback
 978-9916-749-39-5 E-book

KONSENSUS NETWORK

Contents

Publisher's Note

Konsensus Network was founded in 2019 with the purpose of publishing the Finnish translation of The Bitcoin Standard by Saifedean Ammous. We gathered a group of freedom-loving volunteers who were passionate about bitcoin, and we rose to the occasion.

Five years later, and we have expanded from translations to original titles on bitcoin and economics, with nearly 100 books under our belt. We now operate as a hub between authors, license holders, translators, distributors, and production channels.

The next phase in our evolution is to champion freedom, not just bitcoin. This includes the ideals of Austrian economics, libertarianism, privacy, and thought-provoking futuristic fiction.

This book explores time through the lens of fifteen different characters. While we know the timechain as an immutable and very real concept, these stories present alternative universes — alternative ways of thinking. We invite you to free your mind and explore a world where time operates very differently from a chain of blocks published every ten minutes.

– **Niko Laamanen**, *Konsensus Network*

Chapter 1

Invisible Bubbles

Luca Cangemi takes the stage. He sweeps the greying hair out of his eyes and considers the rows of red seats. Before lectures, he still likes to experience the space and imagine his words sailing out to waiting ears. Will this one inspire?

Perhaps it's cliché for a tenured professor to carry a battered leather briefcase, but it has sentimental value. It wears its age like a set of war medals. Since his mother presented it to him at graduation, he's taken it everywhere. As long as he keeps repairing broken straps and clasps, she'll be with him.

He takes in the details of the room – the grain of the wooden lectern, wall lights studded at intervals, that 'new car' smell. Humanities 1 is the biggest lecture theatre in this London university, and this will be the most important lecture of his career.

For a moment, Luca ponders the subject that has consumed his life: the duality of time. For those listening, his lecture will provide some kind of mutual reality, but what does that matter if experience is ultimately individual? He's given hundreds of lectures, thousands maybe. They both inspire and exhaust him. He remembers his student days in Perugia. Gisella. A relationship, a realisation, a beautiful conversation that was both shared and deeply personal. Now he struggles to make small talk with his estranged wife when picking up Alicia.

9:52 am. Someone tries the door. It will remain locked until five minutes before the event. The students attending his first rendition of An Introduction to The Philosophy of Time will come from different disciplines – sciences, the arts. His work draws people together, just as time does. In the next hour, they will learn everything Luca Cangemi knows about the subject, in condensed form.

He spends his last minutes before the doors open dreaming of those two weeks with Gisella.

Luca sets the coffee pot on the stove, then goes back to bed. "It's the afternoon already," he says to the girl looking out of the window.

"And?"

Their scent permeates the room. It is the entire history of their brief relationship.

As a nineteen year-old undergraduate in the old city of Perugia, Luca's lucky to have a studio flat arranged by his aunt. Dark wood, sun-faded wallpaper and zealous pictures of Jesus on the cross. When he moved in, he didn't bring much more than his notebooks and a holdall. He watches Gisella observe the people in the square below. The muscular detail of her back is hidden by a cascade of espresso-black hair. After two weeks of sharing the apartment, Luca is still no closer to understanding what drives her.

"Tell me about this theory again," she says, still gazing at the street.

Luca replies from his side of the crumpled bed. "What I said about the bubbles? It's more of a thought, really."

"Whatever it is, I love it."

"It's that," he says, looking at the ceiling, "time exists in invisible bubbles. Billions of them, which change in shape and size. They can fit inside your head or be as big as the ocean. This is your experience."

Gisella, who is supposed to be in a linguistics lecture, looks over at her young sage. "And this room is the bubble for us?"

Luca wants to say yes. He wants to experience 'oneness' with Gisella and leave the apartment only for pastries and bottles of beer to share, but this visualisation of time occupies him even more than her questions, her secrets, and the scent of the two of them. "Everyone lives a different actuality, so, of the billions of different bubbles, we never exist in the same one."

She turns and asks Luca if they are in the same one when they make love.

Whichever invisible bubble he is in bursts. Whatever he says will be too honest or dishonest, too calculated and scientific or too vague and philosophical. He cycles through his options, calculating how to turn around this chess match from a losing position. The outcome remains the same. Mate.

She pulls on a t-shirt and flicks out her hair. "Really? Not even if we are thinking the same thing?"

Again, he wants to say yes, but instead, he babbles something about shared dreams. He can't even remember where he read the idea about bubbles. The rumble of the coffee pot from the kitchen snaps them out of their individual thoughts, and back into the room.

Gisella walks around the bed, passing under the painting of a wounded Jesus. She stops with her hand on the door. "It's a shame you can't see the bubbles inside the coffee pot when it's hot. You could test your theory."

Luca lies back and smiles.

She opens the door and walks out. The presence of the two of them that was trapped in the sheets and the walls and curtains follows her out into the corridor.

Time elapsed: 80ml of water, evaporated through roasted beans and poured to serve in two tiny cups

Chapter 2

Needle number 1,875

Carly Smith slots into the space at the end of the back row. The packed lecture hall quietens and Luca Cangemi introduces himself. His voice carries a slight accent. She recognises him as the author of that best-selling science book. The last time she attended a talk like this was probably twenty years ago, before she got pregnant and dropped out.

"A trick of the mind, sleight of hand, misdirection, that's all it is," he says.

It's so quiet, Carly wonders if she should hold her breath. Some of the students take notes and underline things.

"You notice how time passes, and that as you get older, you gain experience. Well, in today's lecture, you'll learn that you've spent your whole life looking in the wrong direction, while the universe performs the illusion of time."

It's nice for Carly to do something for herself. Her son, Shaun, doesn't know she's snuck in to learn along with him. There are no checks at the door. Anyone can walk in and expand their mind.

"At school, you were told there are sixty minutes in an hour, a leap year has an extra day, and that a stopwatch can capture a millisecond. But time is much harder to pin down than you think. One theory is that time is merely a dimension that moves while everything else stands still. Some believe it guides us through space from event to event, and this forms our reality. My lecture, for example, will not be over in an hour. It exists in eternity as an event. You just happen to be experiencing it now."

Carly listens, enraptured.

"Presentists believe there is only the now. Eternalists argue that to reveal our full reality would be too much for us and the order of our cosmos would shatter."

Eternalism. Powerful stuff. This is why she came to the lecture. While she listens, time halts and Carly gains control of her life, one event at a time. She's not just a student's mother who works in a factory. She is more than that.

Mechanical sounds echo through the factory, and Carly sits at her workstation threading needles. *Click, clack, click, clack.* This is what she does, thousands of times a day, literally attaching suture thread to surgical hooks. She clocks in, sits down, and four years go by before she can even ask about getting a pay rise.

Megan and Shaun, now teenagers, need bus money and new trainers and reheatable dinners and phone credit, but they'll have to make do with the bare minimum until Carly's next payday. One addiction is replaced by another, so the money always goes. Last time it was joining fees for a multi-level-marketing company. Boxes of cosmetics and nutritional supplements still clog the hall and lounge.

During her break, she talks about that talent show on TV and wrings her hands in want of a cigarette. The room is a windowless office with melamine furniture and a machine that charges for instant coffee. Even the breaks last forever.

At the latest how-to-win-at-life seminar, Carly spent two hundred pounds learning how to take control of time (as if rehab hadn't taught her that). The guy sold everyone on his technique, but was less specific about how to earn money or find happiness.

After fifteen long minutes, Carly goes back to her workstation and attaches a needle: number 1,875. It's amazing that this is the needle that will change everything, not the one that delivered that first hit or the one that gave her Hep C. Machines click and whirr over the sound of radio advertisements. The clamp goes down and the metal hook crimps the green plastic thread, but the electrical counter remains the same: 1,875. And again, for the next one. Is she daydreaming or was the motivational speaker right? This moment, like any, could be the memory of a future her. He claimed that linear time does not exist. The event of needle number 1,875 exists. The tiny pinprick scars on her thumb and index finger exist. And the track marks. It all happens simultaneously and stays there frozen for eternity.

What if Carly could catch the memories from future versions of herself, more successful ones who found love, or run their own company? She could follow the thread back to this present moment.

She looks around the factory floor and sees more individual moments – the new girl swearing at a machine that will be jammed for eternity, the steam hiss of finished items forever sterilised – these are the events through which time flows. Number 1,875 was the needle that punctured time, so Carly can understand she'll always be an addict and will always be clean. She'll always be poor and always be rich. In the next moment, her life will split into a million different pathways and she will experience them all.

Carly Smith sits at her workstation, threading needles.

Time elapsed: nil / infinity

Chapter 3

Time 2.0

Javier Cáceres recognises some of the words displayed on the presentation screen behind the professor: *zaman, vremya, zeit, chronos, hora*. For Javier, this slide makes more sense than the previous ones.

"These," says the lecturer theatrically, "are translations for the most common noun in the English language. They are, of course, words for time." His mid-length grey hair reacts a split second behind the rest of him as if it's always trying to keep up.

Tiempo might be a better expression of time in Spanish, but then again, both words have other meanings. Languages are forests, thinks Javier. Words branch and change, and sometimes they wither and die.

"Calendars are a fairly new invention. Accurate timekeeping arrived in the seventeenth century, yet the way we talk about time developed earlier."

As a physics major, Javier knows that there will always be new discoveries, new details and theories that will shake the world of science. Language can be inaccurate. Apart from learning the lyrics to his favourite punk songs, words are not Javier's strongpoint.

"Our language uses length as a metaphor for time," says the professor, measuring space with his arms. "Others use size. Europeans talk about jumping forward in time, whereas the Aymara people of Bolivia refer to the unseen future as behind them." The lecturer gathers pace as he speaks. He gives examples of how English doesn't have an inflectional future tense, and why foreigners like him still get confused between 'this Wednesday' and 'next Wednesday'. Javier sympathises.

Then, the professor's blue eyes glass over. "As a PhD student in the 1990s, I went on a research trip to the Amazon. Linguistic experts studied the Amondawa, a recently contacted tribe who had no words to define time. Theirs is a language that has never left the rainforest. They have no word for 'minute', no watches or clocks. No age. They base time on happenings like when the river flooded or when the sun will set. Everything about the way they speak of time is relative to their environment. There, in the rainforest, I learned more than I could have ever taught them.'

Javier imagines what time would be like without terms to define it. He has given up taking notes.

Written Communication: Citizen 3409, J. Cáceres

I once carved my imagined birthdate into a tree with a chisel. The term was a concoction of words and symbols. The tree has since been ripped out and fed to the wood chipper. All time-stamped objects are eventually wiped clean.

Words are monitored and scoured for any mention of codes or expressions banned under the Abolition of Temporal Terminology Act. Living with relative concepts – next, since, until – is for the good of all.

I've never known those forbidden words that refer to fragments of astronomical revolutions. Our lives were once chained to these measures. Was Time 1.0 shut off or was it transformed piece by piece?

Before writing this, I camped wild in the forest. There were so many darks and lights I lost count, but my contract to fell dead wood goes on ad infinitum, the only variable being the health of the trees. Sometimes I carve things for others to find, words, thoughts, the beauty of dreams. Soon I must step away from pine-scented mornings and starry nights, so I carve these words in my place. *The point of a dream is that you wake.*

Department of Citizen Observations Report: J. Cáceres, 3409, Log 29-2

New development twenty-nine. Written communication bringing into permanency questions about history and Time 1.0. Subject (young male of higher than average intellect) appears to be unaware of the terminology y**r, d*y, and h**r.

Citizen has reached productivity quota and has not met with any known agitators. Surveillance heightened to level three.

Written Communication: Citizen 3409, J. Cáceres

Will the future consist of more redacted words? The powerful elite who seek immortality will have no need for the words 'never' and 'forever'. For me, the point of a life is that it ends.

When I walked outside the walls of the metropolis, I looked for my tree, but it had been eliminated, cleaved precisely to the root, so it was impossible to distinguish wood from ground.

Surely, the learnings of time and history should remain to protect our planet. Someone must know of Time 1.0. Perhaps all it takes is thought. When I go back into the woods, I will work backwards from Time 2.0

through Time 1.9 and so forth, inventing new terminology. I will speak these ideas and carve them into the thousands of trees that breathe life into the metropolis. They cannot all be disappeared.

Department of Citizen Observations Report: transfer request for J. Cáceres, 3409

Citizen has not met with any known agitators but has not reached the required productivity quota. Desire to create illegal terminology recorded. In order to avoid potential contact with other time historians, transfer to a secure facility is advised.

Time elapsed: **Redacted**

Chapter 4

Jan's Calendar Reminders

[displayed on screen]
"Soooo quick. Can we go again?"
"Thought it would never end."

"One of these quotes comes from my ten-year-old daughter after getting off a rollercoaster," says the professor. "The other is me after the same ride. Can you guess which is which?" Jan squints at the screen from the side of the hall, wishing she could shuffle a few places closer. She remembers back to when her Steven was ten – thirty-odd years ago. They'd had a rollercoaster ride all right.

"Time perception shortens with pleasure or reward, so we underestimate the duration. In fact, I conducted an experiment with my daughter by setting a stopwatch on said rollercoaster. Afterwards, we guessed how long it had taken. She swore it couldn't have been more than one minute."

Jan makes a mental note to go on a rollercoaster. Every day, something new. Besides, she might get a discount now she's a pensioner. She can even do the professor's time experiment. "Perception after trauma is lengthened. At the time, I estimated fairly accurately, ninety seconds, but when I think back to my stomach turning upside down, it felt like it was ninety hours."

Jan knows all about trauma. Suffering in silence through the lies, the stealing, and the failed interventions until she turned Steven in. Returning to finish the degree she started all those years ago was supposed to breathe new life into her, but she comes home each night so tired.

"And it's not only pleasure and pain. Time quickens as you age. To my daughter, a school day is still quite a new experience and feels long, whereas I've done a few."

He's showing off now, displaying photos of him receiving certificates and awards in a gown. "Without novel experiences, the years fly away."

A lump forms in Jan's throat. Mr Luca is right. Steven was locked up three years ago today. She can't keep her life on hold any longer. "Sometimes," says Cangemi, "a change really is better than a rest."

Daily Reminders

- Walk alternative route to uni
- Read in different room, different seat
- Listen to new song from Steven's CDs

Weekly

- Add new picture to photo album
- Cook something for first time. Post recipe in support group
- Challenge: strike up conversation with homeless person
- Write another poem about him
- Visit the beach where S went on day release

End of Term List

- Join new club at the parish hall. Pilates? Bridge?
- Read trashy novel for fun
- Sell his car. Buy something nice at auction
- Get a new look. Nails + cut and colour

Goals

- Put your graduation picture next to his
- Give talk about drugs to schoolchildren
- Do a silent meditation retreat
- Find out inquiry date. Answers?
- Visit churchyard. Clean the headstone
- Read him your poems
- Forgive the guards for their negligence
- Forgive the dose that killed him

- Forgive yourself
- Visit a theme park. Measure time on a rollercoaster

Time elapsed: one eighteen-millionth of the jail sentence a son never finished

Chapter 5

The Afterlife is a Lie…

Cangemi poses questions about belief systems. Does God exist outside of time? Why do some faiths use a wheel not a straight line to represent life? Is time an all-devouring god like Kronos, the Greek deity who swallowed his own children to avoid his fate?

Shaun Smith sits close to the front. He's fourteen rows away from his mother, not that he's seen her. Shaun doesn't care about religion apart from when it stops him getting what he wants. Amanda, who clearly likes him, doesn't believe in sex before marriage. Shaun doesn't have forever. This is university, isn't it? He drifts in and out of the lecture. Most of his brain is occupied with sensations he has not yet experienced.

"Desire to escape the yoke of time pushes many toward religion. Hindus use the cycle of reincarnation while Buddhists maintain that time itself is a form of suffering. The afterlife offers a higher plane where we transcend temporality."

The mention of churches and temples whips Shaun from his day-dream. He scans the hall. Thankfully, Amanda is not taking this class.

"According to the scriptures, the universe and time were created.

However, if this is true, their creator cannot be *in time*, since God existed *before*. And if heaven is eternal, how do we experience time there?"

Shaun is pretty sure he exists in time. About God, he's not certain. He knows his prime pulling days are melting away, like a candle burning down to the nub.

The church is empty. The quiet stills the noise inside Shaun's head. Exam failure, his lack of party funds, the fact he's still a virgin at nineteen, that all stays outside.

He reflects on what Amanda from his psychology class told him about the pleasures of now versus eternal bliss. Shaun watches the dagger rays of red and green light that slice through the window onto pictures of mournful-looking saints. The altar glints a gold-toothed smile.

A low voice breaks the silence. "The afterlife is a lie, you know."

A white-haired man emerges from behind a pillar. The pockmarks on his face are not dissimilar to Shaun's.

"Yeah?"

"But not in the way you think."

Nutjob. Surely.

"I've just come back from there," the man says, staring at his hands, wiggling his fingers in turn. "When you die, time runs out. You can visit paradise once before you go. Only once, mind." He points to the confession booth, which emits a noticeable glow from inside. "It's in there."

Shaun strides over to the booth and opens the door before the man can stop him. He hears a distant shout as he enters.

Golden light rushes into Shaun's body, filling every pore with invincible energy. The old man was right. Shaun is transported directly to heaven.

Soon, an ever-changing string of models occupy the penthouse suite with him. He becomes an expert lover. He plays concerts in the world's best-known clubs. There are no exams and no money troubles. Soon, the buzz wears off, and Shaun gets his thrills by fighting to survive in the only place where he can die – on screen, in a video game. The confession booth gathers dust in the corner of his lounge and over time, its light fades.

But Shaun's blissful life is incomplete. He imagines what his afterlife would be like if he'd entered when he was older, or was African like his granddad, or if he were rich, or a woman, or smarter. Would he still kick back in the gaming chair and watch his enemies' heads explode in ultra-high definition?

Eventually, the fading light of the booth becomes an obsession. What will happen when it shuts off? Opening the door is the only risk left. Shaun misses risks. So, one day, with the recklessness of a teenager, he drops his controller, strides across the room, and enters the portal.

Brilliant light gushes from his body, draining out of every square millimetre of skin. Years of pressure and strain enter his being. Shards of pain pulsate through every joint. He grips the wooden rail and closes his eyes as the trapped light becomes unbearably bright. Muscles waste, skin sags, and his hair greys to white.

Shaun leaves the wooden box and hurries down the church aisle back to his life, but each step is painful and slow. He catches his breath by leaning against a pillar. Despite the pain, it's a relief to be back. The dimensions of the space, the angles of the stonework, the distance of the echoes, the height of the columns, and the hue of stained-glass light are tailor-made to fill the void in Shaun's perfect afterlife.

The entrance door creaks open and a lanky teenager walks into the church. He wears the same kind of skinny jeans and button-down shirt combo Shaun used to. The boy's gaze follows the lines of coloured light from the high window down to the dusty pews.

This time, he will stop himself.

Both Shauns listen to what emptiness sounds like.

Time elapsed: one afterlife

Chapter 6

The Sound of a Crash

On the way to his lecture, a lorry nearly wiped Gareth clean off the planet. He's re-lived it hundreds of times already. His thoughts rattle like loose bearings. Concentrating on the lecture helps him not spiral into 'whys' and 'what ifs'.

Gareth is failing half his modules and only picked philosophy because he thought he could bullshit the long-form exam answers. The reality of reading lists and essay deadlines soon added to the weight of the grey sky pressing down. Perhaps an accident would've been easier.

"Sound is embedded in time." The lecturer enunciates every word like a bell. "It's the primary way we experience the passing of time."

The sound of the lorry's horn will haunt Gareth forever. Even though he's a second-year student, he still feels like he doesn't belong. Should he even be in this lecture? The others are gifted. The others are scribbling notes. He gets anxious in seminars, when ordering lunch, and when he shuts the car door and turns on the engine. The only thing that calms him is ambient music channels and noise-cancelling headphones.

"In one of the great historical theses on the subject, St Augustine uses sound to prove that the past, present and future comprise our experience of time." The professor clicks the controller and religious chamber music seeps out of the wall-mounted speakers. It grows in surround sound and, gradually, the clinical lecture hall transforms into a vaulted, spiritual space.

For a moment, Gareth experiences the calm of a monastery as monks sing long flowing notes. Harmonies rise and fall and intertwine. It's ominously beautiful. The music has the opposite effect to the blare of the horn which jolted him awake. The melodies fade and retract. Gareth is left stranded where they were.

"To enjoy this sound, we need experience – a memory of the notes which led to the current moment. We need attention to process the present sound, and anticipation of the beat, and forthcoming melody."

The choir music returns for a few seconds.

Gareth gauges the distance of each of the speakers and senses how the notes travel through the air, reverberating off walls. He knows music. He listens with his eyes closed, for once not an impostor. Time is just sound over distance, and music is time.

Gareth is alive, he thinks. Car tyres hum in the distance, their destinations meaningless. He can't see; his nose is smashed and his face weeps blood. He tries to imagine the scene. It's night. Something is spinning. Wind buffets the twisted metal but he feels no chill. His brain is a computer programme, desperately searching for micro noises and data to build a picture in time.

"Alright, mate? If you can hear us, we're going to get you out. Sit tight, you've been in an accident."

The voice reminds Gareth of his uncle, a train conductor who always knows where he's going.

The cutting starts and far-off noises mutate into hacking and sparks.

Gareth is awake, briefly. He senses sterile air, distant monitor bleeps, the hospital hum, and the almost imperceptible hiss of the air mattress.

This isn't feeling, but absence, like when your body stops fighting the shock of a cold pool and you dissolve in the water. With your eyes closed, you listen to the bubbles escape. Sound travels faster underwater.

Footsteps tap. Ten yards, then closer. The sound of curtains drawing, the faint singing of the nurse who turns him, washes him, and changes one plastic tube for another. This is his music now. It is his memory, the focus of his attention, and the expectation of days or months of the same.

Sirens sound in the distance, then the window shuts and they retreat.

Gareth is leaving soon. They're finally talking about doing it.

"You know, Deborah, we have to think ab–"

"Don't…"

He's not sure when his parents usually visit, or if they ever leave. They've always shared Gareth's taste in music, to the point they used to tell him to turn his teenage records up, not down. His consciousness (if that's what it is) leaves him with the spacious groans and shallow rasps of the night, but sometimes it returns. Sometimes his parents are there. He's at peace with not being able to communicate. Gareth just listens and his parents just talk.

His dad plays one of his old favourites on the tinny portable speaker they installed. Jimmy Cliff. All the richness of the sound is lost, like it's travelling from another planet.

"This one gets me."

Me too, thinks Gareth. When the singer's voice hits those high notes, the past and the present and future blend into something immense, a feeling worth more than the lives of the three bodies listening.

Gareth hears them shuffle closer. A hand touches his. As the song plays, they make their decision.

Turn the music up, he thinks. Turn it up.

Chapter 7

Time is Money

One day, it will be Angela giving lectures, but, for now, she watches. The way he flows between topics like they were all thoughts born in that order, that's talent. The exact content of today's lecture doesn't interest Angela. She's come to see him in his element, to better understand Luca Cangemi.

"Time was no mystery to early man. We gathered during the day and slept at night. Homo sapiens sensed change and migrated with the seasons."

Angela's PhD thesis is based on the time-perception of mice. It's always mice; they're expendable. Did he see her? Angela slumps in her middle-of-the-row seat. No escape.

"With the formation of civilisations, we began to investigate our senses. Aristotle described time as a 'number of change with respect to before and after'. Only those capable of counting experience it, and if nothing changes, time doesn't pass. It was more than a thousand years before his ideas were proven mistaken."

It's been exactly forty-eight days since the night of the faculty party.

Luca would describe their one-night stand as a mistake. He's still married. He has a daughter; they're always married with kids.

"Newton's principles were based on an external clock of absolute time, which always ticked on regardless of change or perception."

The professor moves along the timeline of great men who contributed to the history of the subject. Always men. Will he become a slide in her lecture some day?

"Since Einstein rebranded time, there have been more discoveries, but really, like with all matters of science, the universe and us, they provide more questions than answers. Some claim that time cannot be universally defined or accurately measured; therefore, it ceases to exist."

Angela looks at the sea of faces around her, drowned in unknowns. She thinks how far she's come since her undergraduate days, only to put her academic career in jeopardy. She should demand the whole row stand up to let her out. She should leave and let him see that she's leaving.

"Now, the grip of appointments and deadlines tightens each day. Is the desire of time to run the economy? If things were different, we might pay for goods with time and not with those meaningless banknotes we call money."

When he strings ideas together, she doesn't mind donating her precious free period to come and watch. But time is something he cannot give her. It's been exactly forty-eight days since they were together. Angela knows, because that's how long the baby has been growing inside her.

Universe 8B. Public transmission: At midnight, Monetary Reform Law comes into effect. From this point, the only legal tender will be Time-Based

Currency (TBC). All electronic funds in other currencies will be converted as per the standardised rate. Please consult your personalised guide on how the Time-Barter System (TBS) affects you.

Angela reads the message, then reads it again. After years of transition, they've pulled the trigger. In four hours, money ceases to exist. It's not that radical when you think about it. Money was crude. Still, the banking system didn't even last a thousand years.

One banknote: worthless.

Her heart pounds and she triple-checks the message. It's tonight. Can it ever be fair, putting a value on a person's life? So many theories swim in her head but one message floats to the top. Midnight. Surely, the elderly will become worthless. And how can you pay back two-thirds of a dead soldier's life?

She weighs up what to do with her last hours of freedom. Ironically, the calculated worth of a philosophy lecturer is low, so contemplation is not profitable in the short or long term. Angela's hours reading the great works and pondering life's bigger questions will not earn her enough minutes to buy essentials for Thomas.

Twenty unbranded nappies: thirty minutes of paper grading.

Angela likes to sing to Thomas, but she'll be more careful from now on. She needs to save up Value Time Transactions (VTTs) minute by minute for the inevitable days lost to hospital appointments and prescription refills. Gazing out at the pounding sea, chopping root vegetables for a stew, a good night's sleep, these are all missed opportunities to grow her worth.

One mother's song to her child: one less pill. Unknown time off his life.

In her academic role, Angela will attempt to study the effects on a representative group. To explain the full TBT computer database and how minutes are taxed from the time-rich would be as complicated as explaining time itself. Society could start again, they said. Equal opportunities and wealth, they said. Yet, when an errant father, a famous time theorist, prefers to maximise VTTs over seeing his sickly son for one minute of a second weekend, the system is broken before it has begun. No matter how many times she reads the message, Angela will not be ready for midnight.

Time elapsed: £4.10 of labour of a tenured university professor

Chapter 8

The Direction of Everything

Luca Cangemi has reached the halfway point of his lecture. As he talks, the professor visualises the months and years mapped out in front of him – office hours, book launches, conferences, more Christmases and birthdays since the separation. The irony that time travels in one direction is not lost on a scholar who can't leave his mistakes in the past. If he were to stand the audience up and switch them around like pieces in a puzzle, would it change the direction of their lives?

"If I asked you to imagine a timeline for the duration of this lecture, where is the start? Over here, yes?" He points to the left of the audience facing him. "But if you came from a Mandarin-speaking culture, you might say up here, above your head. Or if you are from South America, perhaps in front of your eyes."

For Luca, it's the other way around. He can see the future arguments about visiting rights, the unspoken distance between his daughter and him growing, Alicia discussing her overachieving father in therapy.

"Whichever linguistic or spatial properties we apply to time, it only flows in one direction. No matter how much we wish to turn it back, we cannot."

He has seen Angela trying to blend into the middle of her row. All it takes is one momentary lapse in judgement to be ruined in today's academia. It didn't seem wrong at the time, but the guilt eats at him. He must speak with her and clear the air.

"The principles of physics do not rely on the forward motion of time, but the constant increase of disorder does. This is entropy."

Sharing the direction of time is never enough. The dream of proving we can share the experience of time is what drives Luca. He has taught in New York and his native Italy. He has conducted groundbreaking research in The Amazon and is now a professor in London. Sharing in the journey of driven academics like Angela is the reason he still cares about his work.

He steps off stage and seizes a brown paper cup from the front row. "When the coffee gets cold, the heat energy we bought still exists, but in the room, not in the cup. This is a gain in entropy." The coffee he drinks in the faculty cafeteria tastes bitter and stewed. "When the cup sits here long enough, the water will evaporate. This, too, is a gain in entropy."

As he climbs back onstage, he recognises the growing disorder in his life. However carefully he plans things, chaos grows.

Luca Cangemi and everyone he knows will be long dead, but the moment will come. Theoretical physicists believe it will be anywhere from 2.8 to 22 billion years in the future. In that moment, everything reverses.

The Big Crunch is a cosmological event in our future and our past in which the density of matter grows sufficiently that gravitational attraction overcomes the expansion that began with the Big Bang. Entropy reverses and the second law is broken. Chaos retreats.

Order is regained as space contracts.   Broken rocks reform and decayed bodies reanimate. We live our lives in reverse, unexperiencing everything we did the first time around, moving backwards, shrinking towards birth. Instead of questions about creation, we search for the harbinger of order. Who began this? What is our final form?

Luca imagines the crowds at his book signings dissipating and the offices of his academic fellowships decreasing in size. Wrong turns are righted and his family grows closer. His briefcase heals itself and he returns it to his mother. Life rewinds back to him as a young boy, unreading the words that inspired him to look for meaning in all of this. If it can all be reversed, are all shared experiences undone? All bonds broken? Luca returns into his parents, then ancestors, apes, microbes, and nothing. The earth, the planets and stars all merge into one perfectly ordered mass.

Yet, this is not an end, but another beginning in which the universe is reborn in another bang. Galaxies, planets, plants, and philosophy professors will live the same lives as they did billions of years before (and after). The process of positive and negative entropy repeats and we all make the same mistakes again.

Time elapsed: the infinitely repeating cycle of a universe

Chapter 9

Bigger Than, Smaller Than

Some of the minds in the shared space of the lecture theatre process things at a faster pace. English isn't Geeta's first language, but she doesn't get extra time in exams. She's struggling to keep up as the lecturer switches topics. This is supposed to be a philosophy class, but he spends most of the time quoting the laws of physics and psychological studies. Are professors born with brains that go at twice the speed?

"Perception of time depends on scale, with smaller, quicker animals darting to and fro, experiencing a different pace of life to that of a lumbering elephant. Many creatures don't estimate time based solely on circadian rhythms or changes in temperature or pressure. Fish, mice, and even bees can distinguish exact durations as measured by humans. But the fly in your house owes its skill in avoiding rolled-up newspapers to its ability to observe motion on a finer scale than your eyes can achieve, allowing it to cheat death like in the 'bullet time' sequence in *The Matrix*. We often quote the fact that an insect only lives for a few hours, reproducing, then dying. It experiences as full and complete a life as you or me, as measured by its own perception of time."

Geeta puts down her pencil. The mention of the fly transports her to the humid heat of her mother's kitchen in Bangalore. Cumin seeds frying in oil. The sweat on the back of her neck. They toiled for hours in that tiny space, performing the ritual dance of workers in unison. No matter how much Geeta cleaned, there were always flies. No matter how well they cooked, the empty plates returned to the kitchen without real gratitude.

The professor grips the lectern. "One theory suggests the only true measure of time is a life, lived for a distinct duration at a different pace, but experienced the same."

The fly is fading. After each journey, it lands on surfaces thick with grease and smoke. With no time to rest, it surges into sweltering air. It must eat; it must find an exit. A never-ending maze of geometric obstacles form its 360-degree worldview. Again it lands.

A change in air pressure from above. The fly gathers strength, beats its wings, and launches. As it takes flight, an object one hundred times the area of the insect's body smashes down. The fly rides the shock wave up towards the ceiling fan, then dances in and out of the blades, adapting to their rhythm.

Now airborne, the fly senses lumbering movement below. A sudden clattering alerts its antennae. In the air, it is free to twist and turn in dimensions unfathomable to humans. But it cannot fly forever. The insect lands on the curtain rail to rest, its tiny heart pounding at ten beats per second.

"You've gotta hit where it will be, Geeta, not where it is."

She drops the swat and gets back to invigilating the pots on the stove. When you take your focus away for just a minute, hard work gets destroyed.

"Like cricket, yah?" says her younger brother Deepak, peering in from the serving hatch. "Visualise." He closes his eyes and mimics hitting the perfect six over mid-off. Her brother always has some clever remark. "Bigger than, smaller than," he says, practising his English while comparing the size of her samosas. Then he points to his over-inflated head. "Bigger brain, smaller brain." He doesn't know that Maji helps her read books in English so she can get out of the kitchen one day.

The fly dives from the ceiling and rests on a swollen ball of dough.

Geeta usually hates the thought of hurting an animal, but there is nothing she would rather do than smash this one to pulp.

Weighed down by flour granules and oil, exhausted from hundreds of rerouted flights from wall to wall, the fly has no escape.

A change in air pressure. The fly strains, but its body won't respond. Finally, with a huge effort it takes off. For a split second, it tastes freedom in the humid air, then the plastic grill hurtles down and slams its body back to the worktop. A puff of flour rises, then slowly settles on the body. With its wings snapped and thorax caved in, the desperate fly struggles onto weakened legs. It anticipates a change of air, but the swat does not come again. It takes minutes for the insect to expire – weeks in its perception, all the time in the agony of death.

"Faster than, slower than," says Geeta, pointing at the crushed fly. Later she will drop it into Deepak's bed, then she'll read English with Maji for every possible minute before lights out.

Time elapsed:

- *48,000 beats of a broken wing*
- *12 samosas ready to serve*

Chapter 10

Rhythm and Fever

"Hunger, sleep, stress, mood, alertness. We sense time without the clock. These are the internal rhythms of our bodies."

Behind the stage, Cyril listens to the lecture through the partition while he pushes his mop around the battleship-grey floor. Illness, he thinks, that's an important one. He stays fit by wiping the dust that settles each college day.

"Rhythm provides our keenest sense of time, but it cannot be separated from the influence of the outside world. Take the sleep-wake cycle for instance. The distinct corporal region charged with keeping time sits right above the point where the optic nerve fibres cross. Light provides clues. Without it, our circadian rhythms judge days as twenty-five hours, then twenty-six or more."

While he goes back and forth to the bucket, careful not to disturb the students with any knocks or bashes, Cyril thinks how lucky he is to have a job that allows him to just 'be'. He does his work and does it well. Usually, he tunes out of the chatter around him, but this lecture seems tailor-made for him.

"Internal metronomes can change in an instant. Ecstasy, pain, and danger all trigger the release of hormones which alter our perception of time."

Cyril's internal clock is working just fine. To him, consistent balance is life's greatest achievement. He's had his share of stress and pain. Now he fixes things and keeps the place clean.

"The risk of myocardial infarction skyrockets in the week following the daylight saving time shift," says the lecturer. "Biological patterns will always trump the external construct of minutes and seconds. Regular cycles may be one of the most important aspects of overall health."

Cyril hasn't been ill since he was a child, and hasn't missed a shift since his drinking days.

"Time," says the lecturer, "isn't merely a philosophical or physical question, but a biological one too."

Cyril rests his mop against the wall. The floor gleams.

Cyril holds up the stopwatch for his granddaughter to see. "Ten seconds exactly. Told you it's my superpower."

She doesn't believe he can do it again.

"I'll prove it. Been able to count time since I was eight and a half."

His granddaughter looks deep into his eyes. "Same age as me."

Cyril waited to tell her this story for maximum effect. Part of him hopes she'll be able to do the same, but he knows the fever gave him his unique ability.

"Well," he says, "my sense of time broke into little pieces when I was sick with glandular fever. I was in bed for eons but all I could do was count it ten seconds at a time."

The little girl asks questions with her eyes as she listens. Why? How?

"The doctor gave me two weeks off school, which felt like a year. I didn't know day from night, or how long the bowls of cold soup had been sitting there." Cyril's pounding headaches robbed him of his appetite, and the sweat-sodden bedsheets never dried despite his mother propping the window open. The room swirled in a vortex of hours and days without sleep. "The only constant was the swollen bullets in my throat," he says. Little Cyril was terrified.

In his world records book, he once read that the longest a man went without sleep was eleven days. He died after that. Cyril doesn't tell his granddaughter this.

"When the fever finally broke, and I could go outside again, my mother bought me the stopwatch I'd begged her for."

His granddaughter holds the metal stopwatch by its chain. She presses each of the three buttons – Start, Lap, Reset – just as her grandfather did.

Cyril marked the years of school and seven more as an apprentice chippy, then started a family. At twenty-eight, he had a house in a burgeoning neighbourhood, a wife, and two children, but he kept no routines apart from fifteen cigarettes a day, five coffees, and six beers. Anything to alter the monotonous tick inside. Coffee turned to pills and beer turned to whisky.

One day the foreman told them to stay off site. One of the lads had fallen from the fourth floor and impaled himself on an upright rebar. No wrongdoing, he misjudged the edge of the concrete while swinging a sledgehammer. Bad timing.

Cyril didn't have to discuss it with anybody but himself. He gave up drinking, caffeine and nicotine. Eventually, he gave up construction too.

"You can't outrun your own sense of rhythm," he says. "Your body is the most important thing to listen to."

His granddaughter, hearing nothing, moves close, virtually sitting in Cyril's lap. She presses her ear to his barrel chest to catch the beating of his heart. She seems disappointed by its normality. To her, Cyril is just her dad's dad, able to perform a funny magic trick on command. "Do it again, Granddad. And no peeking."

Cyril presses start, and for exactly ten seconds, the girl's eyes don't leave the stopwatch.

Time elapsed: one hundred and seventy beats of a 63-year-old male's heart

Chapter 11

The Grand Clock of Total Order

Cangemi still hasn't replied to Katy Weller's query about her last essay score. She's only permitted one fifteen-minute tutorial per week, but it's not like there's a line of students waiting to get in. What do her tuition fees actually pay for? Arriving early and sitting in the front row was the only way to make sure she could grab a minute with him after the lecture.

"All this is very well," he says, "but why do we experience time?" A pause. "In a word, survival."

This makes total sense to Katy's scientifically wired mind. To propagate life, species must store memories and project behaviour. That way they can make the right choices. Katy likes to think she makes good choices for her future. She wants to publish research, not hide from curious minds in a cosy office.

"Yet humans have expanded their memories and projections to a level beyond survival. Time is purely emotional to us."

Katy is less sure about this part. She writes down a few questions and hopes there will be a chance to ask them.

The professor scratches his head and continues as though he is letting everyone into a big secret. "We use so much time-based data to inform our decisions, we've become scared of death, not focused on survival."

This might be so, but with each step of her life meticulously planned, Katy can achieve great things. After a masters, a doctorate, and becoming the head of a global research company, she'll make real change. Her mates would tell her to be impulsive and carefree like them. But she doesn't have mates.

"An interesting question persists. What if our universe is merely a part of a bigger construct, experiencing time and emotions foreign to us? This might sound fanciful, but it's something that can never be disproved."

Katy is fine with the idea that her plan and her universe is part of something greater. On her notepad, she writes the words 'universe' and 'clock' with an equal sign between them. A question mark is added.

The numbers are undeniable. Kate Weller grips the desk, trying to ground herself while the permutations and combinations fire through her mind like loose electrons. She thought she would scream, dance in joy, run into her team's office and share the news. Something stops her.

Through the collection of radio-telescope data, Kate's team has correlated the movement of over two hundred galaxies. Waiting for the huge numbers of independent studies to report back has been like watching far-off planets spin helplessly on their own axes. Now the model is complete. On the screen in front of her, Kate sees the bigger picture and feels crushed by the perfection of its total order. A lump builds in her throat. For once, her heart is full.

The speed of orbits, trajectories of celestial bodies, the distances between spiralling masses all correlate in fractal beauty. Kate understands that rather than forming part of a bigger picture, they are movements in a massive machine.

Apart from her work, she has nothing to lose – an expensive apartment with never-worn party dresses and an empty fridge. Here is the paradox: her life has led to this discovery, but presenting the universe as a time-keeping mechanism will strip her of all credibility. After years of waiting for the stars to align, there is no one with whom to share the beauty.

She starts to format an email entitled 'Project Radio Findings'. All Kate needs is a way to sell the idea to pique the interest of the institute board. Once they see the patterns she does, they'll surely grant her the next round of funding. On screen, the cursor blinks.

Yes, there are anomalies, blips in the data, but these could simply be swells and draws of emotion, subject to an invisible biological force. Could the universe be a particle in a multi-dimensional brain?

The sprawling pot plant in the corner of her office always calms her. Kate runs her fingers through its jagged leaves. If plants and humans can connect, why not something bigger?

In the next thirty minutes, Kate types out the top-line findings. Until now, she never knew she could compress years of research into a convincing one-page argument. Is it convincing? She deletes the text and tries again. And again. The afternoon passes.

By eight pm, she has it. Her finger hovers over the send button. There's no going back from proposing an answer to the true meaning of the Cosmos. It will occupy the rest of her career, but the battle for proof will never complete her as much as that first look at the results.

In the time it takes to weigh up her options, she contemplates how minute this decision is in the grand scheme – pot plants, cities, planets, galaxies, universes are all interconnected moving parts in something unimaginably great.

Time elapsed: an infinitesimal measurement of one of the billions of components in the grand clock of total order

Chapter 12

Post-Trip Diary

The professor moves on to the effects of drugs. Eve wonders if he's ever taken anything – probably, but not in the way she has. Narcotics are a learning tool for Eve, like info-dense lectures and errors in judgement. She looks around. All these people could learn a thing or two about drugs.

The professor explains the effects of psychedelics on time. Stimulants activate dopamine and alcohol dulls your senses, but LSD, mushrooms, DMT, they unlock something. He describes a study of forty people on doses of twenty micrograms of psilocybin. They measured dots appearing on a computer screen and blah, blah, blah. Eve knows the script of these sterile experiments. They're always inconclusive, and advise more caution and more expensive studies. Funny that.

"One thing to understand about psychedelics experiments," he says as though he's just dropped a couple of tabs at a house party, "is their purpose is not to measure how these chemicals 'destabilise' our bodies."

Eve doesn't 'experiment' with drugs, contrary to her flatmates' jokes. She welcomes them like old friends, makes time for new experiences, invites them back for coffee instead of nightclub knobheads.

"In his book *The Doors of Perception*, Aldus Huxley describes an experience of mescaline where duration is replaced by the perpetual present. The drug added layers of extra-real perception."

An urge builds inside her. She's not trying to ruin the guy's lecture, just, for some reason, Eve can't hold it in. Before she can stop herself, she shouts, "Anyone got any mescaline?"

Heads turn, lots of them.

The professor looks up, but sees an empty space where Eve's voice was. She's ducked into the footwell behind the solid desk. Cangemi peers at the troublesome empty seat, then carries on with his lecture.

"A bet with your mind." That's what it is, according to Jim Morrison. Swallow a tab and there's no going back. No why or what comes next.

This time, Eve has hidden the clocks, completed reaction tests on a website and rigged up a camera. She remembers Johnny Depp in *Fear and Loathing*. Now it's her in a hotel room with nothing but a microphone and her own fucked-up sense of reality.

Post-Trip Diary: Watching the webcam video feels wrong. There is a CCTV version of me who knows exactly where she is, but is completely lost...

Space blends and curves. Eve becomes a sort of non-self. The tabs she bought from Nav are strong. The poster of an all-seeing eye on her wall fires rays of red, but she's not here to document visuals and shooting colours. She tries to mark time, but her spidery handwriting transforms to coded pictures on the page.

The girl in the video goes at eight times speed. Time passes around her. She is a ghost, staring into the soul of the wall, looking for answers. A curl of hair wraps around her finger over and over. 01:20, she talks into the dictaphone. The recordings are garbled messages about the one night she wishes she could get back...

How long's it been? The dark house gives no clues. Anyone could burst in, even Nav. That night comes back each trip. Good hook-ups aren't easy to find; Eve keeps buying and he keeps dancing around the issue.

For around two hours, I offer myself to a string of updating moments, but at 03:05 a look takes hold. 'That night' has arrived. You can chase the everlasting present, but the past catches up with you eventually. It was easier to give in than pay my debt to Nav, then it wouldn't be rape in the back of a Ford Fiesta and I wouldn't be damaged.

Eve completes the computer tests again with similar results. It's wearing off. She's not tired, so she watches videos about the effects of LSD and the life of Aldus Huxley. Then, the coloured lines recede and she powers down. Can any other twenty-year-olds say they've journeyed as deep as her? Before sleep, she orders a copy of The Doors of Perception. Apparently, it's how Jim Morrison chose the name for his band.

Time elapsed: 87 times the duration of the sexual assault that cleared a drug debt

Chapter 13

High Altitude

"You'd think that here, in this space, we share time, but it's more complicated."

Another problem. Ray thought philosophy would require a bit of mental agility, not the bloody-mindedness to wade through streams of heavy equations. When this lecturer was on that TV show, the topic seemed much simpler.

"Due to gravitational warping, altitude causes a measurable change in the passing of time." As he speaks, Cangemi traces the lines of seats in the auditorium, from his level all the way up past Ray's row. "For example, if one twin spent seventy-nine years living one metre higher than her sister, the first woman would end up approximately thirty billionths of a second older."

Ray has a twin, sort of. The young guide he met on his gap year in Bolivia was called Ramón. They had loads in common, even though the other Ray came from a little village 4,000 metres above sea level. "Even in our world, governed by standardised zones and calibrated clocks, we can never truly experience the same time as each other."

The students alongside Ray are shuffling their pens and papers into some kind of obstacle course. How is Ray supposed to figure out which assignment he can best answer, if he can't even concentrate on the lecture? From the corner of his eye, he sees the reason for the distraction. An ant explores the long writing platform in front of the seats. It zigs and zags to avoid the pencils, mobile phones, and sweet wrappers dropped in its path. At the same time, the professor explores the stage, pacing up and down, left and right.

"Going back to our twins, consider the effect of the difference a millisecond in their lives may cause: perhaps nothing, perhaps everything."

The ant scurries toward Ray. He brushes the insect onto the floor and wonders if they have the same problems in Bolivian universities.

A baby is born to wealthy parents in a coastal town in England. Everyone in the town is wealthy, so the boy never feels blessed. In his teens, he becomes curious about money and life and equality and what it all means. He takes a gap year to do charity work.

While teaching English at a school in the high Andes, he meets a tour guide of the same age with the same name. They laugh, learn, and share stories. When they play football, the altitude sucks the life out of one of them. He still thinks about his Bolivian friend, but they lost touch when he returned to England.

One day, on a long drive home with his family, a tightness in his chest causes the man to stiffen at the wheel and lose control. He veers left, then right. In the flash of the moment, he flings the car to the side, avoiding the back of a lorry by millimetres. The car spins to a stop on the hard shoulder. The children in the back seat cry; his wife sits in shock, open mouthed. He grips the wheel and takes a moment to ground himself.

After this, the man takes care of his health, works hard, leads a moral life, stays married, and watches his children grow up in a seaside town where everyone else is rich, so they don't feel blessed.

A baby is born in a poor neighbourhood in a Bolivian mountain town. Everyone in the town lives in poverty, so the boy never feels deprived. In his teens, he befriends an English teacher who shares his name. When they see how he laughs and jokes with the foreigner, jealous locals leave him out of the neighbourhood football games. He loses contact with the teacher, but continues working as a tour guide.

Although he never leaves his town, he earns enough to move to a better house, marries, has children, and meets many more foreigners who puff and wheeze on their way up the mountain.

One day, the man's family are on the long drive back from the capital. It's dark and he nods off at the wheel for a split second. A grip around his heart jolts him awake and he pulls the wheel hard to the left. The jeep veers and spins. In the beam of the headlights, he sees the black shape of the truck a millisecond too late. He takes the impact. A flash of light. When he comes to, his leg is broken, his wife is screaming, and the children are silent.

He's too late to save his car, his leg, his job, his house, his children, his marriage. Every day, he sits in his parents' old house, looking down on the newer part of the city, watching the neighbourhood children playing football. He thinks about money and life and death and fairness and what it all means.

Time elapsed: 0.0000001 seconds more of age

Chapter 14

Cocktails at the Pioneer Café

Tom was desperate to be an astronaut when he was young. Desperate. He sits close to the exit with his bag packed, just as he did in school, as if he might get the call from the space agency at any moment. He told his friends his father was an astronaut, even though he'd never met him.

The lecturer's talking about space travel now. He always uses relatable examples: coffee cups, twins, the Moon. So many nights Tom stared up and asked if his father really was out there and if he would ever come back.

"A moving clock will appear to tick slower than a clock at rest in your frame of reference. The faster the velocity, the greater the time difference." He pauses to allow the note-takers to catch up. "At the speed of light, the tick of the moving clock slows to zero."

The speed of light is something Tom knows off the top of his head. After his boasts of spacewalks and a visit to Cape Canaveral, some of the boys in his class joked that his father fled at 299,792,458 metres per second and was never seen again. Tom stopped wanting to be an astronaut. When people have asked about his old man since then, he's shrugged.

"Every year, I get asked the same questions about time travel. It's actually quite annoying."

Tom burrows down in his chair. His surroundings collapse into a black hole, same as when the joke about his father did the rounds at school. He was *that* student, the time travel guy. His eyes shift towards the exit, as if it has the ability to teleport him somewhere better.

"But it *is* possible in a way. After six months on the International Space Station orbiting the planet at a speed of about 7,700 metres per second, an astronaut will age about 0.005 seconds less than those on Earth."

Relief – all those childhood films weren't complete lies. If his father ever returns, Tom will be the one who has travelled forward in time, and his dad will still be the same guy that left twenty years ago.

Tom knew his father would be late, but he's sat there watching the door like some southern belle, waiting for Daddy to return from battle. This is not Tennessee; he's in the Pioneer Café, section 15B of Capital Station, Mars. His father has already been away ten Earth years, so why not wait a little longer?

The airlock opens for what feels like the hundredth time and his father is standing there with the same yellow teeth and the same Stellar Transit uniform – a traveller from the past. Tom wonders whose hair is greyer now. It takes the man a couple of laps around the café before he notices Tom. As he approaches, his bootsteps barely sound in the pressurised café hub.

"Son," he says.

At least it wasn't a question. Tom waits for more small talk but he comes up empty.

"I'll get us a cuppla Doghouse Brews, eh, Tommy Boy?"

That ratty unfiltered stuff was banned under the last health mandate. Of course, he wouldn't know that. Tom tells his father he could do with something to fill him out, and orders two protein cocktails on the console. One minute of awkward silence later, they arrive. His father takes a sip and stares with eyes so hollow Tom's not sure if he's lost all sense of taste or if he's gotten better at masking his disgust.

"Got any news for me?" he asks, as though his son has been saving up pictures of the grandkids and writing him a card each holiday.

Tom asks him how long he's back for.

"Ten days," he says, then sips his pink drink, this time pulling a face. He can't decide what's worse, the drink or time off the ship. He's lost muscle. Maybe he's sick. Maybe it's bad this time.

The airlock opens and the last remaining customers walk into the tunnel, back to their lives furthering the reaches of the human race. Now, it's just the two of them, the hiss of the ventilation system and two protein cocktails sitting on the cold steel table.

Tom considers asking him about his job, about the things he's seen, about how it feels to see pioneers age like they're stuck in fast forward. Really, he wants to ask why his dad brought him to this ugly rock as a kid and accepted a job that took him as far away as possible. Maybe Tom should ask him why he missed Doghouse Brew more than he missed his family. But, he doesn't. Those questions will still be there in another ten years.

After a few more minutes ignoring his drink, something fires up his father's blue-flame eyes. He undoes the top button on his uniform and asks, "You wanna know what it's like to travel at the speed of light?"

Time elapsed: 1/7th of a life. 1/70th of a life

Chapter 15

The Definition of Now

Professor Luca Cangemi begins the conclusion of the one-hour talk containing his life's work. He holds his Swiss watch to his ear. It's such a precision instrument, he can't hear the faintest tick.

"The Julian calendar was mandated in 46 BC," he says. "Horologists produced the first pendulum clock less than four hundred years ago. GMT arrived in 1880, then came atomic time precision and even recalibrating 'leap seconds'. Yet, time is still inaccurate."

For a moment, he pauses, drinking in the expectation of the audience. That little four-letter word consumes him every second of every day. Perhaps it does for some of them too. In this long moment of reflection, the watch remains clamped to Luca's ear. He listens to its non-tick.

"The answer to the riddle of time is not a destination. It's a journey you have to take on your own."

The digital bell sounds three times, hanging in the air like dots between one hundred and eighty possible realisations.

Luca stiffens. There's a space. Just one. It's a gap which any of the minds present could occupy given enough shuffling around. Cangemi pictures the audience as one of those 'fifteen puzzles' – a four-by-four block of slidable pieces with one empty square. It took Bobby Fischer just seventeen seconds to solve one on Carson in 1972. It's taken Cangemi seventeen years to see it clearly.

He looks longingly at the space. It contains a different approach to solving the paradox of time. He could quit teaching, start again and focus more on enjoying the present moment. Breaking his pattern of error and regret fills him with the kind of excitement he's not experienced since those two coffee-stained weeks with Gisella.

From the looks on some of their faces, Luca can tell there is an epiphany coming to them. The empty space is the missing piece that could make them all happy —- the girl who demands two tutoring sessions per week, the tall kid with acne scars, the mature student sitting off to the side, and this year's 'time travel guy'. And Angela. Whatever Angela wants, he will make time for her after the lecture because she deserves more than a letter of recommendation and an awkward kiss on the cheek goodbye.

Finally, he speaks. "I hope that this talk has inspired you to think about your relationship with time." He smiles. "For what is life without it?"

The bell sounds again and the exodus begins.

Before considering amendments to the universally agreed laws of time, the Council of Time chair gives a full reading of the term in question: " 'Now' is an adverb identically defined in most languages. It refers to a conscious present moment relative to any individual who thinks, believes, utters or writes it."

One Luca Cangemi, Professor of Philosophy, born AD 1972, approaches the council to state his case. "My motion to change the definition of 'now' is not based on scientific proof, but on shared emotion."

Despite vehement disagreement from Sir Newton, the man's right to speak is upheld.

Cangemi cuts a curious figure. His Italian suit exudes quality, but he wields a tatty briefcase. Despite his racing heart, he speaks to the council in a sombre, measured tone.

He cites the audience of his last lecture as proof that it's possible to share the emotional state of 'now'. A moving permutation of listeners with car-crash nightmares, brilliant futures, painful losses and missing afterlives shared the space of his epiphany.

"In a public moment of discovery," he says, "realisations can be accessed. Others in the room who process their own seismic changes may share my eureka at a later point. And when they remember back to this moment of clarity, they experience the same change. The same *now*."

Mr Aristotle notes that change is critical to time, so 'now' could exist outside individual consciousness. The council chair asserts that Cangemi must provide some kind of further proof of the 'common now'.

Luca Cangemi approaches the bench. His blue eyes display no emotion, but a whole world burns within them. "Look, and you will see my 'now'." He holds the gaze of the large ticking clock above the council bench. "You share in this epiphany. I am here by thought alone, outside the bounds of time, but inside the bounds of now."

The absence of an application to appear before the council prior to Mr Cangemi's visit confirms this as fact.

The greatest scientists in history peer deep into the man's eyes. They see those in the lecture hall who realise their need to understand time's questions and answers. They see the students' past and future, their beauty and pain. They see Luca Cangemi, a father again, attempting to balance family and his career. They see his acceptance of his journey. The men see themselves amending the definition of 'now'.

One by one, they corroborate the philosopher's evidence and vote unanimously in favour of changing the law.

Cangemi holds the amendment in his hand. " 'Now,' " he says, "refers to an individual or shared conscious present moment, relative to those who think, believe, utter or write it." This is the little piece of happiness he discovered in the empty space of a packed lecture theatre.

Immediately after he reads the definition, a kaleidoscope mixture of brilliant colour and vacuum black, of interstellar velocity and glacial change, transmits Luca Cangemi back to Humanities 1.

He sweeps the greying hair from his eyes and stares at the rows of empty seats. The clock reads nine-fifty-five. Time has transported him here, past everything else important in his life. Time has changed him, and he has changed it.

Luca Cangemi breathes in the car-fresh smell of the clean seats. He imagines the words of his new definition sailing out to waiting ears.

The doors open and the unsuspecting epiphanies rush in.

Time elapsed: now

About The Author

Philip Charter is a totally human writer, laser-focused on spreading the gospel of bitcoin and cypherpunk ideals. He is the editor of the 21 Futures anthology series and has published four books of short fiction. After leaving the UK to search for more sun, he now resides in Gran Canaria, Spain.

Made in the USA
Las Vegas, NV
08 December 2024

13594614R00059